Dear Kara & Tim,
May these fairy tales
inspire your little girl's dreams
and imagination throughout
her childhood!
Love,
Lori Trotta

Classic
Fairy Tales

Classic Fairy Tales

Illustrated by
Scott Gustafson

ARTISAN

NEW YORK

These pictures are for Karl.—S.G.

Library of Congress Cataloging-in-Publication Data
Classic fairy tales / illustrated by Scott Gustafson.
p. cm.
Audience: "Ages three & up"—Jacket.
Summary: An illustrated collection of ten traditional fairy tales, including "Goldilocks and the Three Bears,"
"Puss in Boots," "Little Red Riding Hood," "Snow White," "Tom Thumb," "Hansel and Gretel,"
"The Frog Prince," "Rumplestiltskin," "Cinderella," and "Three Pigs."
ISBN 978-1-57965-686-7
1. Fairy tales. [1. Fairy tales. 2. Folklore.] I. Gustafson, Scott, ill.

PZ8.C5573 2003
[398.2]—dc21
2003049197

SOURCES CONSULTED

The Golden Goose Book, L. Leslie Brooke. Copyright 1905 Frederick Warne & Co.; *Perrault's Fairy Tales*, translated by A. E. Johnson, illustrated by Gustave Doré. Copyright 1969 Dover (Translations from *Old-Time Stories Told by Master Charles Perrault*, translated by A. E. Johnson. Copyright 1921 Dodd Mead & Company); *Blue Fairy Book*, Andrew Lang. Copyright 1889 Longmans, Green, and Co.; *Fairy Tales Every Child Should Know*, edited by Hamilton Wright Mabie. Copyright 1905 Doubleday; *Household Stories* by the Brothers Grimm, Lucy Crane. Copyright 1886 Macmillan and Company; *Favorite Fairy Tales*, illustrated by Peter Newell. Copyright 1907 Harper & Brothers; *English Folk and Fairy Tales*, collected by Joseph Jacobs. No copyright indicated. G. P. Putnam's Sons; *Fairy Tales of the Brothers Grimm* by Mrs. Edgar Lucas. Copyright 1911 Selfridge & Co. Ltd.; *English Fairy Tales*, Flora Annie Steel. Copyright 1946 Mabel H. Webster; *Folk-Lore and Fable*, The Harvard Classics, Vol. 17. Copyright 1909 P. F. Collier & Sons.

Design by Sheryl P. Kober

Artisan books are available at special discounts when purchased in bulk for premiums
and sales promotions as well as for fund-raising or educational use. Special editions or book
excerpts also can be created to specification. For details, contact the Special Sales Director
at the address below, or send an e-mail to specialmarkets@workman.com.

Published by Artisan
A division of Workman Publishing Co., Inc.
225 Varick Street
New York, NY 10014-4381
artisanbooks.com

Published simultaneously in Canada by Thomas Allen & Son, Limited

Printed in China
23 22 21 20 19 18 17   2014 2015 2016

Contents

Goldilocks
and the Three Bears

Once upon a time there were Three Bears, who lived together in a house, in a wood. One of them was a Little, Small, Wee Bear; and one was a Middle-Sized Bear; and the other was a Great, Huge Bear. They each had a bowl for their porridge—a little bowl for the Little, Small, Wee Bear; and a middle-sized bowl for the Middle-Sized Bear; and a great bowl for the Great, Huge Bear. And they each had a chair to sit in—a little chair for the Little, Small, Wee Bear; and a middle-sized chair for the Middle-Sized Bear; and a great chair for the Great, Huge Bear. And they each had a bed to sleep in— a little bed for the Little, Small, Wee Bear; and a middle-sized bed for the Middle-Sized Bear; and a great bed for the Great, Huge Bear.

One day, after they made the porridge for their breakfast and poured it into their bowls, they walked out into the wood while the porridge was cooling, so they wouldn't burn their mouths by beginning to eat it too soon.

In a village, just beyond the forest, lived a little girl who loved to run through the long grass, picking wildflowers. Her hair fell in golden locks about her shoulders, so everyone called her Goldilocks.

This morning, however, Goldilocks wandered too far, and before she realized it, she found herself deep in the shadowy wood. Soon, she came upon the Three Bears' cottage. Glad to find a house in the middle of the forest, she ran from window to window and peeked in. Seeing no one at home, she went to the door and tried the latch.

Now, the Three Bears, who themselves were very polite creatures, never thought that anyone would come into their house without an invitation, so they always left their door unlocked. But Goldilocks, who was sometimes so curious she forgot her manners, opened the door and invited herself in.

The moment she smelled the cooling porridge, Goldilocks remembered how hungry exploring the forest had made her. If she had waited for the Three Bears to come home, she might have been invited for breakfast, for they were good-natured bears and hospitable. But, instead, she decided to help herself.

First she tasted the porridge of the Great, Huge Bear, but that was too hot for her. And then she tasted the porridge of the Middle-Sized Bear, but that was too cold for her. And then she went to the porridge of the Little, Small, Wee Bear and tasted that; and that was neither too hot nor too cold, but just right, and she liked it so well that she ate it all up.

Then Goldilocks sat down in the chair of the Great, Huge Bear, but that was too hard for her. And then she sat down in the chair of the Middle-Sized Bear, but that was too soft for her. And then she sat down in the chair of the Little, Small, Wee Bear, and that was neither too hard nor too soft, but just right.

So she seated herself in it and there she sat until the poor little chair broke into pieces and down she came—plump!—upon the ground. Then Goldilocks went upstairs into the bedrooom where the Three Bears slept. And first she lay down upon the bed of the Great, Huge Bear, but that was too high at the head for her. And next she lay down upon the bed of the Middle-Sized Bear, but that was too high at the foot for her. And then she lay down upon the bed of the Little, Small, Wee Bear, and that was neither too high at the head nor at the foot, but just right. So she covered herself up comfortably and lay there until she fell fast asleep.

By this time, the Three Bears thought that their porridge would be cool enough to eat, so they came home to have their breakfast. But things were not how they had left them.

Looking into his bowl, the Great, Huge Bear said in his great, huge voice, "SOMEBODY HAS BEEN TASTING MY PORRIDGE!"

Then the Middle-Sized Bear said in her middle-sized voice, "SOMEBODY HAS BEEN TASTING MY PORRIDGE!"

And the Little, Small, Wee Bear cried, "Somebody has been tasting my porridge, and has eaten it all up!"

Then the Great, Huge Bear looked at his chair. "SOMEBODY
HAS BEEN SITTING IN MY CHAIR!"

And the Middle-Sized Bear said, "SOMEBODY HAS BEEN
SITTING IN MY CHAIR!"

And the poor Little, Small, Wee Bear cried, "Somebody
has been sitting in my chair, and has broken it all
to pieces!"

Then the Three Bears thought that they
should make a further search of the
house, so they went upstairs into
their bedroom.

Goldilocks had pulled the pillow of the Great, Huge Bear out of its place.

"SOMEBODY HAS BEEN LYING IN MY BED!" said the Great, Huge Bear, in his great, rough, gruff voice.

And Goldilocks had also pulled the pillow of the Middle-Sized Bear out of its place. "SOMEBODY HAS BEEN LYING IN MY BED!" said the Middle-Sized Bear, in her middle-sized voice.

And when the Little, Small, Wee Bear came to look at his bed, there was the pillow in its place, and upon the pillow was the head of Goldilocks—which was not in its place, for she had no business there.

"Somebody has been lying in my bed, and here she is!" said the Little, Small, Wee Bear, in his little, small, wee voice.

Goldilocks had heard in her sleep the great, rough, gruff voice of the Great, Huge Bear and the middle-sized voice of the Middle-Sized Bear, but it was only as if she had heard someone speaking in a dream. But the little, small, wee voice of the Little, Small, Wee Bear was so sharp and so shrill that it woke her at once.

Up she started, and when she saw the Three Bears on one side of the bed, she tumbled out the other side and ran to the window. The window was open, because the Three Bears, being good, tidy bears, always opened their bedroom window in the morning. Out Goldilocks jumped and ran away as fast as she could run—never looking behind her. What happened to her afterward I cannot tell, but the Three Bears never saw anything more of her.

The End

Puss in Boots

A certain miller had three sons, and when he died, the only worldly goods that he had left to them were his mill, his donkey, and his cat. This little legacy was very quickly divided up. The eldest son took the mill, and the second son took the donkey. All that remained for the youngest son was the cat, and he was very disappointed to receive such a miserable portion.

"My brothers," he said, "will be able to get a decent living by joining forces, but for my part, as soon as I have eaten my cat and made a fur cap out of his skin, I am bound to die of hunger."

These remarks were overheard by Puss, who pretended not to have been listening, and who said very soberly and seriously, "There is not the least need for you to worry, Master. All you have to do is to give me a pouch and get a pair of boots made for me so that I can walk in the woods. You will find then that your share is not so bad after all."

Now, this cat had often
shown himself capable of performing
clever tricks. When catching rats and
mice, for example, he would hide himself nearby their food and hang downward
by the feet as though he were dead.

His master, therefore—though he did not build too much on what the
cat had said—felt some hope of being assisted in his miserable plight.

When his master gave Puss the pair of boots that he had asked for, Puss
gaily pulled them on.

Then Puss hung the pouch around his neck and, holding the cords that tied it in front of him with his paws, he went into a warren where a great number of rabbits lived.

Placing some bran and lettuce in the pouch, he stretched himself out and lay as if he were dead. His plan was to wait until some young rabbit, unlearned in worldly wisdom, should come and rummage in the pouch for the food that Puss had placed there.

Hardly had he laid himself down when things began to happen as he wished. A stupid young rabbit went into the pouch, and Puss, pulling the cords tight, caught him in an instant.

Well satisfied with his capture, Puss departed to the king's palace. There he demanded an audience and was ushered upstairs. He entered the royal apartment and bowed deep before the king.

"I bring you, Sire," he said, "a rabbit from the warren of the marquis of Carabas" (such was the title he invented for his master), "which he asked me to present to you on his behalf."

"Tell your master," replied the king, "that I thank him and am pleased by his attention."

Another time, the cat hid himself in a wheat field, with the mouth of his bag wide open. Two partridges ventured in and, by pulling the cords tight, he captured both of them. Off he went and presented them to the king, just as he had done with the rabbit from the warren. His Majesty was even more pleased by the pair of partridges and handed the cat a present for himself.

For two or three months, Puss went on in this same way, every now and again presenting to the king, as a gift from his master, some new type of game that he had caught.

There soon came a day when Puss learned that the king intended to take his young daughter, who was the most beautiful princess in the world, for a carriage ride along the riverbank.

"If you will do as I tell you," said Puss to his master, "your fortune will be made. You have only to go and bathe in the river at the spot that I will point out to you. Leave the rest to me."

His master had no idea what the cat was planning, but he did just as Puss directed.

While he was bathing, the king drew near, and Puss at once began to cry out at the top of his voice, "Help! Help! The marquis of Carabas is drowning!"

When he heard these shouts, the king stuck his head out of the carriage window. He recognized the cat who had so often brought him gifts and he asked his guards to go immediately to help the marquis of Carabas.

While the guards were pulling the poor marquis out of
the river, Puss approached the carriage and explained to the king
that while his master was bathing, robbers had taken away his clothes,
although he had cried, "Stop, thief!" at the top of his voice. But, as a
matter of fact, the clever cat had hidden the clothes under a big stone.

The king at once commanded the keepers of his wardrobe to select
a suit of his finest clothes for the marquis of Carabas.

The king greeted the marquis with many compliments and, as the fine
clothes that the marquis had just put on made him look like a gentleman and
set off his good looks (for he was very handsome), the king's daughter found
him very much to her liking.

Indeed, the marquis of Carabas had not cast more than two or three tender glances upon her when the princess fell madly in love with him. The king then invited the marquis to get into the coach and ride with them.

Delighted to see that his plan was beginning to work so successfully, the clever cat went ahead of the coach. Soon, he came upon a group of peasants who were mowing a field of wheat.

"Listen, my good fellows," he said, "if you do not tell the king that the field that you are mowing belongs to the marquis of Carabas, you will all be chopped up into little pieces like mincemeat!"

Soon, the king arrived and he asked the mowers who owned the field on which they were working.

"It is the property of the marquis of Carabas," they all cried in one voice, for the threat from Puss had frightened them terribly.

"You have inherited a fine estate," the king said to the marquis.

"As you see for yourself, Sire," he replied, "this is a meadow that never fails to yield an abundant crop each year."

Still traveling ahead of the others, Puss came upon some harvesters.

"Listen, my good fellows," he said, "if you do not declare that every one of these fields belongs to the marquis of Carabas, you will all be chopped up into little bits like mincemeat!"

The king came by a moment later and wished to know who owned the fields he saw before him.

"It is the marquis of Carabas," cried the harvesters.

At this the king was more pleased than ever with the marquis and he complimented him on his many noble possessions.

Traveling ahead of the coach, Puss made the same threat to all the people he met, and the king was astonished at the great wealth of the marquis.

Finally, Puss reached a splendid castle that belonged to a giant ogre. He was the richest ogre that had ever been known, for all the lands through which the coach had passed, and which the king admired, were part of the castle's domain.

The cat had taken care to learn everything he could about the ogre and what powers he possessed.

Puss now asked to speak with the ogre, saying that he did not wish to pass so close to the castle without having the honor of paying his respects to the owner. Puss entered a large room, where the ogre received him as politely as an ogre could and invited Puss to sit down.

"I have been told," said Puss, "that you have the power to change yourself into any kind of animal that you would like to—for example, I have heard that you can transform yourself into a lion or an elephant."

"That is perfectly true," said the ogre sternly, "and just to prove it to you, I will immediately turn into a lion."

Puss was so frightened to suddenly find himself so close to a lion that he sprang away and climbed onto the roof of the castle—but not without much difficulty and danger, for his boots were not well suited for walking on roof tiles.

Some time later, when the cat saw that the ogre had changed himself back from a lion, Puss climbed down from the roof, admitting that he had indeed been very frightened.

"I have also been told," Puss said to the ogre, "but I can scarcely believe it, that you have the power to take the shape of even the smallest animals— that you can change yourself into a rat or a mouse, for example. I must confess that to me that seems quite impossible."

"Impossible?" cried the ogre. "Well, you shall see right away!" And at that very instant, the ogre changed himself into a small mouse, and began to run about on the floor to every corner of the room. No sooner did Puss see the tiny mouse than he pounced on it and ate it.

In the meantime, the king came along and, admiring the ogre's beautiful estate, ordered his coachman to drive up to the gate, as he wished to visit the castle.

The cat heard the rumble of the coach as it crossed the castle drawbridge, and running out to the courtyard, he cried out to the king, "Welcome, Your Majesty, to the castle of the marquis of Carabas!"

"What's that?" cried the king. "Is this splendid castle also yours, marquis? I have never seen anything more grand than this building and courtyard and grounds around it. No doubt the castle itself is just

as magnificent on the inside. With your permission, marquis, may we go inside and look around?" The marquis gave his hand to the young princess as she stepped out of the coach, and followed by the king, they led the way up the great staircase. As they entered the large hall, they found there a magnificent feast that had been prepared by the ogre for some friends who were to pay him a visit that very day. When these guests heard that the king, the princess, and a great marquis were already inside the castle, they did not dare to enter and instead they turned away and left.

The king was now quite charmed with the excellent qualities and the great wealth of the marquis of Carabas, and the young princess was also completely captivated by him. In fact, she had fallen deeply in love with him.

When they had finished eating the great feast, and the king and the princess were quite satisfied with the banquet, the king turned to the marquis and said, "It will be your own fault, marquis of Carabas, if you do not soon become my son-in-law."

The marquis, bowing very low, and with a thousand expressions of gratitude and respect, accepted the great honor that the king bestowed upon him. That very same day, the marquis married the princess, and everyone celebrated with another grand feast. The princess and the marquis made much of Puss, who was treated as a guest of honor at the wedding table.

The marquis promised Puss a comfortable life at the castle for the rest of his life. Puss became a personage of great importance and gave up hunting mice, except for his own amusement.

The End

Little Red Riding Hood

There was once a sweet little maid, much beloved by everybody, but most of all by her grandmother, who could not do enough for her. She gave the girl a hooded cape of red velvet and, as it was very becoming and she never wore anything else, people called her Little Red Riding Hood.

One day her mother said to her, "Come, Little Red Riding Hood, here are some cakes and a jug of cider to take to Grandmother. She is weak and ill, and they will do her good. Hurry before it grows hot, and walk properly and nicely and don't run, or you might fall and break the jug of cider, and there will be none left for Grandmother. And when you go into her room, don't forget to say, 'Good morning,' instead of staring all around you."

"I will be sure to take care," promised Little Red Riding Hood. Now, the grandmother lived deep in the wood, half an hour's walk from the village. When Little Red Riding Hood had reached the wood, she met the wolf; but she did not know what a bad sort of animal he was, so she did not feel frightened.

"Good day, Little Red Riding Hood," he said.

"Thank you kindly, Wolf," she answered.

"Where are you going so early, Little Red Riding Hood?"

"To my grandmother's."

"What are you carrying in your basket?"

"Cakes and cider. We baked yesterday, and my grandmother is very weak and ill, so they will do her good and strengthen her."

"Where does your grandmother live, Little Red Riding Hood?"

"A quarter of an hour's walk from here. Her house stands beneath the three large oak trees, and you will easily know it by the hazel bushes," said Little Red Riding Hood.

The wolf thought to himself, "This tender young thing would be a delicious morsel and would taste better than the old one. I must manage somehow to get both of them."

He walked next to Little Red Riding Hood a little while, and then he said, "Little Red Riding Hood, just look at the pretty flowers that are growing all around you, and I don't think you are listening to the song of the birds. You are walking along just as if you were going to school, and it is so delightful here in the wood."

Little Red Riding Hood glanced around her, and when she saw the sunbeams darting here and there through the trees and the lovely flowers everywhere, she thought to herself, "If I take a fresh bouquet to my grandmother, she would be very pleased." So she ran about in the wood, looking for flowers. And as she picked one, she saw a still prettier one a little farther off, and so she went farther and farther into the wood. But the wolf went straight to the grandmother's house and knocked at the door.

"Who is there?" cried the grandmother.

"Little Red Riding Hood," the wolf answered, "and I have brought you some cake and cider. Please open the door."

"You can open it," cried the grandmother. "I am too weak to get up."

So the wolf opened the door and went right in. Without saying a word, he walked to the bed and ate up the poor grandmother in an instant, for he had been more than three days without food. Then he put on her nightclothes, lay down in her bed, and drew the curtains around him.

Little Red Riding Hood was all this time running about in the wood among the flowers, and when she had gathered as many as she could

hold, she remembered her grandmother and set off again on the path to
her house.

When she arrived at the cottage, she was surprised to find the front
door standing open, and when she went inside, she felt very strange and
thought to herself, "Oh dear, how uncomfortable I feel today, and at other
times I am always so happy to visit my grandmother!"

And when she said, "Good morning, Grandmother," there was no answer.

Then Little Red Riding Hood went over to the bed and slowly drew
back the curtains. There lay the grandmother with her nightcap pulled down
over her eyes, so that she looked very odd.

"Oh, Grandmother, what large ears you have!"

"The better to hear with, my dear."

"Oh, Grandmother, what great eyes you have!"

"The better to see with, my dear."

"Oh, Grandmother, what large hands you have!"

"The better to hold you with, my dear."

"But, Grandmother, what a terrible large mouth you have!"

"The better to eat you with!"

And no sooner had the wolf said this than he made one bound from the bed and swallowed up poor Little Red Riding Hood.

Then the wolf, having satisfied his hunger, went to sleep and began to snore loudly. A hunter passing by heard the snoring and thought, "How the old woman snores! I had better see if there is anything the matter with her."

Then the hunter went into the bedroom, walked over to the bed, and saw the wolf lying there, fast asleep.

"At last I find you, old beast!" he said. "I have been looking for you for a long time." And the hunter suddenly realized that the wolf had swallowed the grandmother whole and that she might yet be saved.

So he did not fire his gun, but took a pair of shears and began to slit open the sleeping wolf. When he made a few snips, he saw the little red cap, and after a few more snips, Little Red Riding Hood jumped out and cried, "Oh dear, how frightened I have been! It is so dark inside the wolf."

And then out came the old grandmother, still living and breathing. Little Red Riding Hood went and quickly fetched some large stones, with which she filled the wolf's body, so that when he woke up and tried to rush away, the stones were so heavy that he sank down and fell dead.

They were all three very pleased. Little Red Riding Hood and her grandmother thanked the hunter, who then returned to his hunting in the forest. The grandmother ate the cakes and drank the cider and began to feel much better. Little Red Riding Hood said to herself that as long as she lived, she would never leave the path and stray about in the wood alone, and she would always do exactly what her mother told her.

The End

Snow White

Once upon a time, in the middle of winter, when the flakes of snow fell like feathers from the sky, a queen sat at a window set in an ebony frame, and sewed. While she was sewing and watching the snow fall, the queen pricked her finger with her needle, and three drops of blood dropped on the snow. And because the bright crimson looked so beautiful on the white snow, she thought, "Oh that I had a child with skin as white as snow, lips as red as blood, and hair as black as the wood of this ebony frame."

Soon afterward, the queen had a little daughter, who had skin as white as snow, lips as red as blood, and hair as black as ebony, and she was called Snow White. But when the child was born, the queen died.

After a year had gone by, the king took another wife. She was a handsome lady, but she was proud and haughty, and could not bear to think that anyone could surpass her in beauty.

This queen had a wonderful mirror, and
each time she looked into it, she would say:
"Mirror, Mirror, on the wall,
Who is the fairest of us all?"
And the mirror would answer:
"Queen, thou art the fairest of them all."

And the queen was satisfied, for she knew the mirror always told the truth.

But Snow White was growing ever taller and prettier, and grew to be as beautiful as the day, and more beautiful than the queen herself. So one day, when the queen asked of her mirror:

"Mirror, Mirror, on the wall,

Who is the fairest of us all?"

The mirror answered:

"Queen, thou art the fairest here I hold,

But Snow White is fairer a thousandfold."

The queen was startled, and turned yellow and green with envy. From that hour, her heart turned against Snow White and she burned with secret hatred whenever she saw the young girl. Pride and envy grew like weeds in her heart until she had no rest day or night.

At last, the queen called a hunter and said to him, "Take the child out in the forest, for I can no longer stand to have her in my sight. Kill her, and then bring me her heart as proof that you have done it."

The hunter obeyed, and led the child away. But when he drew his hunting knife, and was about to pierce Snow White's innocent heart, she began to weep, and said, "Ah, dear hunter, spare my life, and I will run deep into the wild forest, and never come home again."

The hunter took pity on her, because she was so lovely, and said, "Run away then, poor child!"

"The wild beasts will soon make an end of her," he thought to himself, but it seemed as if a stone had been rolled away from his heart, because he had not taken Snow White's life. As a little bear came by just then, he killed it, took out its heart, and carried it to the castle as proof to the queen.

The poor child was now all alone in the great forest, and as she looked at all the leafy trees, she felt frightened and did not know what to do. So she began to run, and ran over the sharp stones and through the thorns; and the wild animals passed close to her, but they did not harm her. She ran as long as her feet could carry her, and, when evening closed in, she came upon a little house, and went into it to rest.

Everything in the house was very small, but I cannot tell you how pretty and clean it was! There stood a little table, covered with a white tablecloth, on which were seven little plates (each plate with its own little spoon)—and seven little knives and forks, and seven little cups.

Against the walls stood seven little beds close together. Snow White was very hungry and thirsty, so she ate a little of the vegetables and bread on each plate, and drank a drop of water from every cup, for she did not want to empty one cup entirely.

Then, being very tired, she laid herself down in one of the beds, but she could not make herself comfortable, for one was too long, and another too short. The seventh bed, luckily, was just right. So there she stayed, said her prayers, and fell asleep.

When it had grown quite dark, the masters of the house came home. They were seven dwarfs, who dug and mined iron underground among the mountains. They lit their seven candles, and as soon as the house became bright they could see that someone had been there, for everything was not quite as orderly as they had left it.

The first dwarf said, "Who has been sitting on my stool?"

The second one said, "Who has been eating off my plate?"

The third one said, "Who has been nibbling my bread?"

The fourth one said, "Who has been eating my vegetables?"

The fifth one said, "Who has been using my fork?"

The sixth one said, "Who has been cutting with my knife?"

The seventh one said, "Who has been drinking out of my cup?"

Then the first dwarf looked about, and saw that there was a slight hollow in his bed. He said, "Who has been lying in my bed?" Five others came running, and each called out, "Someone has been lying in my bed, too!"

But the seventh, when he looked in his bed, saw Snow White lying there, fast asleep. He called the others, who gathered around the bed with cries of surprise, then fetched their candles, and cast the light on Snow White.

"Oh, good heavens!" they cried. "What a lovely child!" And they were so pleased that they did not wake her, but let her remain asleep in the little bed. The seventh dwarf slept with all of his companions in turn, an hour with each, and so they passed the night.

When it was morning, Snow White woke up, and when she first saw the seven dwarfs, she was frightened. But they were very friendly and asked her name in a kind way.

"Snow White," she answered.

"How have you found your way to our house?" asked the dwarfs.

So she told them how her stepmother had tried to kill her, how the hunter had spared her life, and how she had run the whole day through, until at last she had found their little house.

Then the dwarfs said, "If you will keep our house, cook, make the beds, wash, sew and knit, and keep everything neat and clean, you can stay with us, and you shall want for nothing."

"I will, with all my heart," said Snow White. So she stayed with them and kept their house in order. Every morning, they went out among the mountains, to seek iron and gold, and came home ready for supper in the evening.

The young girl was left alone all day long, so the good dwarfs warned her, "Beware of your wicked stepmother, who will soon find out that you are alive. Be sure not to let anyone into the house."

Now the queen, believing that Snow White was dead, had no doubt that she was again the first and fairest woman in the world. So she walked up to her mirror and asked:

"Mirror, Mirror, on the wall,

Who is the fairest of us all?"

And the mirror replied:

"Queen, thou art the fairest here I hold,

But Snow White, over the seven hills,

Who with the seven dwarfs now dwells,

Is fairer still a thousandfold."

The queen trembled, knowing the mirror always told the truth. She felt sure that the hunter had deceived her, and that Snow White was still alive. She thought and thought, late and early, early and late, how best to kill Snow White. For her jealous heart would give her no rest until she again was the fairest lady in all the land.

At last the queen thought of a plan. She painted her face, dressed herself like an old peddler woman, and changed her appearance so much that no one could recognize her. In this disguise, she went over the seven hills, until she came to the house of the seven dwarfs. She knocked at the door and cried, "Fine wares to sell! Fine wares to sell!"

Snow White looked out of the window and said, "Good morning, good woman. What have you to sell?"

"Good wares, fine wares," answered the queen, "ribbons of all colors." And she drew out one that was woven of brightly colored silk.

"I may surely let this honest woman in!" thought Snow White. So she unfastened the door and bought herself some pretty ribbons.

"Child," said the old woman, "what a sight you are! Let me lace your bodice properly." Snow White, fearing no harm, stepped in front of the old woman and allowed her to fasten her bodice with the new ribbon.

But the old woman laced so quickly and so tightly that it took Snow White's breath away, and she fell down as if dead. "Now I am the fairest at last," said the wicked queen to herself, and then she sped away.

The seven dwarfs came home soon after, and they were struck with horror to find their poor Snow White lying on the ground—as if she were dead! They lifted her up, and seeing that she was laced too tightly, they quickly cut the ribbon of her bodice. Snow White began to breathe faintly, and slowly she returned to life.

When the dwarfs heard all that had happened, they said, "The old peddler woman was none other than the wicked queen. You must be very careful, Snow White, and never again open the door if we are not at home."

As soon as the wicked queen returned to the castle she went to her mirror and asked:

"Mirror, Mirror, on the wall,

Who is the fairest of us all?"

And the mirror answered, as usual:

"Queen, thou art the fairest here I hold,

But Snow White, over the seven hills,

Who with the seven dwarfs now dwells,

Is fairer still a thousandfold."

When the queen heard this, she was so alarmed that all the blood rushed to her heart, for she knew at once that Snow White was still alive.

"This time," she said to herself, "I will think of a plan that will make an end to her once and for all."

With the help of witchcraft, in which she was very skillful, the queen made a poisonous comb. Then she changed her face and clothes again, and took the form of a different sort of old woman.

Again she crossed the seven hills to the home of the seven dwarfs, knocked at the door, and called out, "Fine wares to sell!"

Snow White looked out of the window and said, "Go away. I cannot let anyone into the house."

"But surely you are allowed just to look!" answered the old woman, and she drew out the poisonous comb and held it up. The girl was so pleased with the pretty comb that she let herself be tempted, and opened the door.

After Snow White purchased the comb, the old woman said, "Now I will comb your hair properly."

Poor Snow White did not know she was in danger, and she let the old woman begin. But the comb had scarcely touched her hair before the powerful poison began to work, and Snow White fell down senseless.

"There, you paragon of beauty!" said the wicked woman. "This is the end of you." And she quickly went away.

Luckily, it was near evening and the seven dwarfs soon returned home. When they again found Snow White lying lifeless on the ground, they at once suspected her wicked stepmother. They searched, and found the poisonous comb, and as soon as they removed it, Snow White came to herself and told them what had happened. Again, the dwarfs told her she must be careful, and to never open the door to anyone.

When the queen reached home, she stood before the mirror and asked:

"Mirror, Mirror, on the wall,

Who is the fairest of us all?"

The mirror answered:

"Queen, thou art the fairest here I hold,

But Snow White, over the seven hills,

Who with the seven dwarfs now dwells,

Is fairer still a thousandfold."

When the queen heard the mirror's reply, she quivered with rage. "Snow White shall die," she cried, "even if it costs my own life!"

Then she went to a secret and lonely chamber, where no one would ever find her, and there she made a deadly poisonous apple. Ripe and rosy, it was so beautiful to look upon that anyone who saw it would long to eat it, but whoever might eat even a little bit of it was certain to die.

When the apple was ready, the queen painted her face, disguised herself as a peasant woman, and again journeyed over the seven hills to the house of the seven dwarfs.

When the old woman knocked at the door, Snow White put her head out of the window, and said, "I cannot open the door to anybody. The seven dwarfs have forbidden it."

"Very well," replied the peasant woman. "I only want to be rid of my apples. Here, I will give you one of them!"

"No!" said Snow White. "I cannot take it."

"Are you afraid of being poisoned?" asked the old woman. "Look here. I will cut the apple in two, and you can eat the rosy side, and I will eat the white."

Now, the fruit was so cleverly made that only the rosy side was poisonous. Snow White longed to bite into the pretty apple; and when she saw the peasant woman eat her half, she could resist no longer, but stretched out her hand and took the poisonous half. No sooner had she tasted the fruit than she fell lifeless to the ground.

The wicked queen, laughing loudly, glared at
Snow White with a terrible look and cried, "Oh, you with
skin as white as snow, lips as red as blood, and hair as black as
ebony, the seven dwarfs cannot bring you back to life this time!"
When the queen arrived home, she again asked her mirror:
"Mirror, Mirror, on the wall,
Who is the fairest of us all?"
The mirror at last answered:
"Queen, thou art the fairest of them all." Then her jealous
heart had as much peace as a jealous heart can ever know.

When the dwarfs came home in the evening, they found Snow White lying breathless and motionless on the ground. They feared that indeed she was dead. They lifted her up, searched to see whether she had anything poisonous about her, loosened her dress ribbons, combed her hair, and washed her with water, but all was in vain, for they could not bring the darling girl back to life. They laid her down, and all seven dwarfs sat themselves around her, and they wept and mourned for three long days. Then they would have buried her, but she still looked so fresh and alive, and had such lovely rosy cheeks. "We cannot lower her into the dark earth," they said.

So they had a coffin of glass made for her, so that she could be seen from every side. They laid her in it, writing her name on the outside in letters of gold, telling that she was the daughter of a king. Then they placed the coffin on the mountainside above, and one of them always stayed by it and guarded it. But there was little need to guard it at all, for even the wild animals came and mourned for Snow White. The birds came, too—first an owl, and then a raven, and last of all, a little dove.

Snow White lay in her coffin unchanged for many long, long years. She looked always the same, as if she were asleep, for she still had skin as white as snow, lips as red as blood, and hair as black as ebony.

Then one day, the son of a king wandered into the forest, and he came to the dwarfs' house looking for a night's shelter. He saw the coffin on the mountainside, the beautiful Snow White within it, and he read what was written there in letters of gold. Then he said to the dwarfs, "Let me have the coffin! I will give you whatever you ask for it."

But the dwarfs answered, "We would not part with it for all the gold in the world."

"I beg you to give it me, for I cannot live without seeing Snow White, and, although she is dead, I will prize and honor her as my dearest treasure."

Then the good dwarfs took pity on him and gave him the coffin, and the prince asked his servants to carry it away. As they were going along, they stumbled over a bush, and the shaking forced the bit of poisonous apple out of Snow White's mouth. Immediately, she opened her eyes, raised the coffin lid, and sat up, alive once more.

"Oh, heavens!" she cried. "Where am I?"

The prince answered joyfully, "You are with me," and he told her what had happened, saying, "I love you more dearly than anything else in the world. Come with me to my father's castle, and be my wife."

Snow White agreed and happily went with him, and their marriage was celebrated with great splendor. The wicked stepmother was also invited to the feast. When she had dressed herself in her most beautiful clothes, she stood before the mirror, and asked:

"Mirror, Mirror, on the wall,

Who is the fairest of us all?"

The mirror answered:

"Queen, thou art the fairest here I hold,

But the young queen over the mountains old,

Is fairer still a thousandfold."

The evil-hearted woman uttered a curse, and was beside herself with anger and disappointment. At first, she thought she would not attend the wedding, but her curiosity would not allow her to rest. She decided to travel to the wedding, to see the young queen who the mirror had said was the most beautiful in all the world.

When the wicked queen got there and found Snow White alive again, she choked with her rage and fell down dead.

Snow White and the prince lived happily ever after, and often visited the seven dwarfs, who had been so kind to her.

The End

Tom Thumb

At the court of great King Arthur, who lived, as we all know, when knights were bold, and ladies were fair indeed, one of the most famous of men was the wizard Merlin. Never before or since was there such a wizard. All that was to be known of wizardry he knew, and his advice was always good and kindly.

One day, when Merlin was traveling disguised as a beggar, he happened upon the house of an honest farmer and his wife, who, after giving him a hearty welcome, cheerfully offered him a big wooden bowl of fresh milk and some coarse brown bread on a wooden platter.

Although the man and the woman, and the little cottage where they lived, were neat and tidy, Merlin noticed that neither the husband nor the wife seemed very happy. When he asked them why, they said it was because they had no children.

"If only I had a son, even if he were no bigger than my good man's thumb," said the poor woman, "we should be quite content."

Now, this idea of a boy no bigger than a man's thumb so tickled Wizard Merlin's fancy that he promised the man and his wife right away that such a son should come in due time to bring the good couple much happiness.

He then went off at once to pay a visit to the queen of the fairies, as Merlin felt that the little people would best be able to carry out his promise.

And, sure enough, the very idea of a little man who was no bigger than his father's thumb tickled the fairy queen, too, and she set about the task at once. Soon, the good couple was blessed with the tiniest of little boys.

The parents were now very happy, and the christening of the little fellow took place with great ceremony. The fairy queen, attended by her company of elves, was present at the feast. She kissed the little child, and, giving him the name of Tom Thumb, told her fairies to fetch the tailors of her court, who dressed her little godson exactly as she asked.

His hat was made of a beautiful oak leaf, his shirt of a fine spider's web, and his leggings and jacket were of thistledown. His stockings were made with the rind of a delicate green apple, and the garters were two of the finest little hairs imaginable, plucked from his mother's eyebrow, and his shoes were made from the skin of a little mouse. When he was dressed in his new clothes, the fairy queen kissed him once more, and, wishing him all good luck, flew off with the fairies of her court.

As Tom grew older, he became very amusing and full of tricks, so his mother was afraid to let him out of her sight. One day, while she was making a batter pudding, Tom stood on the edge of the bowl, with a lighted candle in his hand, so that she might see that the pudding was properly made. Unfortunately, when her back was turned, Tom fell into the bowl, and his mother, not noticing he was missing, stirred him into the pudding.

Then she tied the bowl in a cloth, and put it into a pot of boiling water. The batter filled Tom's mouth and prevented him from calling out, but he had no sooner felt the hot water than he kicked and struggled so much that the pudding jumped about in the pot. His mother, thinking the pudding was bewitched, was nearly frightened out of her wits. She pulled the bowl out of the pot, ran with it to her door, and gave it to a tinker who was passing by.

The tinker was very grateful for the pudding and looked forward to having a better dinner than he had enjoyed for many days. But his pleasure did not last long, for, as he was climbing over a fence, he happened to sneeze very hard, and Tom, who had been quite quiet inside the pudding for some time, called out at the top of his little voice, "Bless you!"

This so terrified the tinker that he flung down the pudding and ran off as fast as he could. The bowl was broken in pieces, and Tom crept out, covered with batter, and ran home to his mother, who had been looking for him everywhere and was delighted to see him again. She gave him a bath in a cup, which soon washed off all the pudding, and he was none the worse for his adventure.

A few days later, Tom and his mother went into the fields to milk the cows, and, fearing Tom might be blown away by the wind, his mother tied him to a sow thistle with a little piece of thread.

While she was milking, a cow came by and bit off the thistle, and the thread—and Tom! Poor Tom did not like the cow's big teeth and he called out loudly, "Mother, Mother!"

"But where are you, Tommy, my dear Tommy?" cried his worried mother, wringing her hands.

"Here, Mother!" Tom shouted. "Inside the red cow's mouth!"

And, saying that, Tom began to kick and scratch until the poor cow was nearly mad, and he finally tumbled out of her mouth. His mother rushed to him, caught him in her arms, and carried him safely home.

Some days later, Tom's father took him to the fields to plow and gave him a whip, made of barley straw, with which to drive the oxen. But little Tom was soon lost in a furrow. As usual, birds followed the plow that morning, looking for freshly unearthed grubs, or some other tiny creatures to eat for breakfast. One happened to be a nearsighted hawk, who, mistaking Tom for a plump toad, seized him and flew off over the treetops.

It was only after Tom called out
that the bird realized his mistake, and having
no interest in making a meal of a boy, he let
Tom fall. Below, a giant was getting some air on
the roof of his castle tower when Tom landed on his head.
The giant raised his great hand, expecting to catch a pesky fly, but,
finding something that smelled like human flesh (one of his favorite meals),
he simply dropped poor Tom into his mouth, like a piece of candy.

In a moment, the giant was sorry he had tried to make a snack of the little human. Tom kicked and scratched more wildly than he had in the mouth of the cow. With a mighty spit, the giant sent him flying again through the air, over the battlements and down into the sea.

No sooner had he hit the water than a big fish swallowed him up. This very well may have been the end of Tom Thumb, but nearby fishermen caught the great fish and took it to the royal kitchen.

Imagine the cook's astonishment when he opened the fish and
out jumped little Tom Thumb! Soon, Tom had the whole kitchen
staff laughing wildly at his jokes and pranks. And what is more,
he soon became a favorite of the whole court. When the king
went out riding, Tom sat in the pocket of his waistcoat,

ready to amuse lords and ladies, the king and queen, and all the great knights
of the Round Table.

Tom soon began to miss his parents and begged the king to allow him
to go home for a short time. The king readily agreed and told Tom he could
take with him as much money as he could carry.

Tom had to rest more than one hundred times along the way, but, after two days and two nights, he reached his father's house in safety. His mother ran to meet him, and there was great rejoicing at his arrival. He spent three happy days at home and then set out for the castle once more.

One day, shortly after his return, Tom displeased the king, and fearing the royal anger, he crept into an empty flowerpot, where he lay for a long time.

At last Tom ventured to peep out, and, seeing a fine, large butterfly on the ground nearby, he climbed out of his hiding place, jumped on its back, and was carried up into the air. The king and the nobles all tried to catch him, but at last poor Tom fell from his seat into a watering pot, in which he almost drowned. Luckily, the gardener's child saw him and pulled him out. The king was so pleased to have Tom safe once more that he forgot to scold him and made much of him instead.

As a token of his fondness for the mischievous Tom, the king ordered the court tailor to make a wonderful little suit of clothes. The royal harness maker made a tiny saddle and bridle that transformed a castle mouse into a miniature charger. And so, with a needle from the queen's own sewing basket for his sword, Tom Thumb set forth in quest of another adventure.

Afterward, Tom lived many years at the castle and became one of the best beloved of King Arthur's knights.

The End

Hansel and Gretel

ear the borders of a large forest, there once lived a woodcutter and his wife, who had two children—a boy named Hansel and his sister, Gretel. The family was very poor and had little to live on, and once when there was a dreadful famine in the land, the woodcutter could not earn sufficient money to buy enough for the family to eat.

One evening, after the children had gone to bed, the parents sat talking together about their troubles. The poor husband sighed, and said to his wife (who was not the mother of his children but their stepmother), "What will become of us? I cannot earn enough to support myself and you, much less the children. What shall we do with them, so that they do not starve?"

"I know what to do, Husband," she replied. "Early tomorrow morning, we will take the children for a walk across the forest and leave them in the thickest part. We will light a fire and give each one a piece of bread. Then we

will leave them alone. They will never find the way home again, you can be
sure of it, and then we shall only have to work for ourselves."

"No, Wife," said the man, "that will never do. How could I find it in
my heart to leave my children all alone in the forest, where the wild animals
would come quickly and eat them?"

"Oh, you fool!" the wife said. "If you refuse to do this, you know we will all four die of hunger. You may as well go out and cut the wood for our coffins." And after this, she let him have no peace until he agreed with her plan. That night, he could not sleep for hours, but lay thinking in sorrow about his children.

The two children, who were too hungry to sleep, were also awake and heard all that their stepmother had said to their father. Poor little Gretel wept bitter tears as she listened, and said to her brother, "What is going to happen to us, Hansel?"

"Hush, Gretel," he whispered. "Don't be so unhappy. I know what we can do." Then they lay quite still until their parents were asleep.

As soon as the house was quiet, Hansel got up, put on his little vest, unfastened the door, and slipped out. The moon was shining brightly, and the white pebble stones that lay outside the cottage door glistened like new silver money. Hansel stooped down and picked up as many of the pebbles as he could stuff into his little coat pockets.

Then he went back to Gretel and said, "Don't worry, my dear little sister. Sleep in peace. Heaven will take care of us." Then Hansel laid himself down again in his bed, and slept until morning came.

As soon as the sun rose, the stepmother hurried to wake the two children, and said, "Get up, you lazybones, and come into the forest with me to gather wood for the fire."

Then she gave each of them a piece of bread, and said, "You must keep that to eat for your dinner, and don't quarrel over it or eat it too soon, for you will get nothing more."

Gretel put both pieces of bread in her apron, because Hansel's pockets were already full of white pebbles. Then the stepmother led them into the

forest. They had gone but a short distance when Hansel stopped and turned to look back at the house, and this he did again and again.

At last, his stepmother said, "Why do you keep staying behind and looking back so?"

"Oh, Mother," said the boy, "I can see my little white cat sitting on the roof of the house, and I am sure she is crying for me."

"Nonsense," she replied. "That is not your cat. It is just the morning sun shining on the chimney."

But Hansel had seen no cat. He had stayed behind each time to drop a white pebble from his pocket on the path as they walked along.

When they reached a thick and dark part of the forest, their stepmother said, "Come, children, gather some wood, and I will make a fire to warm you, for it is very cold here."

Hansel and Gretel did as they were told and soon made quite a high heap of brushwood. Their stepmother lit the pile of wood, and it blazed up into a bright fire.

Then the woman said to them, "Sit down, children, and rest, while I go find your father, who is cutting wood in the forest. When we have finished our work, we will come and fetch you."

Hansel and Gretel sat by the fire, and when noon arrived, they each ate the bread that their stepmother had given them for their meal.

From deep in the forest, they heard the sound of strokes of an axe. The children felt safe, for they believed that their father was chopping wood nearby. But it was not the sound of an axe they heard—it was only the sound of a branch that still hung on a withered tree, and was moving up and down in the wind.

Finally, after they had been sitting there a long time, the children began to grow tired, their eyes began to close, and they soon fell fast asleep. When they awoke, it was dark night, and poor Gretel began to cry, and said, "Oh, Hansel, now how shall we find our way out of the wood?"

Hansel comforted his sister. "Don't be afraid," he said. "Let's just wait a little until the moon rises, and then we shall easily find our way home."

Very soon, the full moon rose and Hansel took his little sister by the hand. The white pebbles, which glittered like bright coins in the moonlight, and which Hansel had dropped as he walked into the forest, showed them the way. They walked all night long, and did not reach their father's house until the break of day.

They knocked at the door, and when their stepmother opened it, she exclaimed, "You naughty children, why have you stayed so long in the forest? We thought you were never coming back!"

But their father was overjoyed to see them, for it broke his heart to think that they had been left alone in the dark wood.

Not long after this, there was another season of famine, and the children again heard their stepmother talking to their father at night, after they were in bed.

"The times are as bad as ever," she said. "We have just half a loaf of bread left, and when that is gone, we have no hope. The children must go away. We will take them deeper into the forest this time, and they will not be able to find their way home as they did before. It is the only way to save ourselves from starvation."

But the husband felt heavy at heart, for he thought it was better to share his last morsel with his children. His wife would listen to nothing he said, and continued to scold and argue with him. And because he had given in to her the first time, he could not refuse to do so now.

The children were awake, and heard the conversation. So, as soon as their parents were asleep, Hansel got up. He wanted to go out and gather some more bright pebbles to drop as he walked, to mark the way home, but his stepmother had locked the door, and he could not open it.

When he went back to his bed, he again told his little sister not to fret, but to go to sleep in peace, for he was sure they would be taken care of.

Early the next morning, the stepmother came and pulled the children out of bed, and, when they were dressed, gave them each a piece of bread for their afternoon meal—smaller pieces than they had been given before. Then they started on their way into the forest.

As they walked, Hansel, who had the bread in his pocket, broke off little crumbs and stopped every now and then to drop one, turning around as if he were looking back at his home.

"Hansel," said the stepmother, "what are you stopping for? Come along!"

"I saw my pigeon sitting on the roof, and he
wants to say good-bye to me," replied the boy.

"Nonsense," she said. "That is not your pigeon. It is only the
morning sun shining on the chimney."

But Hansel did not look back anymore. He simply dropped
pieces of bread behind him as they walked through the wood. This time, they
went on until they reached the thickest and densest part of the forest, where
they had never been before in all their lives. Again they gathered a great
mound of brushwood, and the stepmother made a large fire.

Then she said to them, "Stay here, children, and rest, while
I go to help your father, who is cutting wood. When you feel
tired, you can lie down and sleep for a while. We will come and
fetch you in the evening, when your father has finished his work."

So the children remained alone. At midday, Gretel
shared her piece of bread with Hansel, for he had scattered
his own along the road as they walked. They slept for a while,
and the evening passed, but no one came to fetch the poor children.

When they awoke, it was still quite dark, and poor little
Gretel was afraid. But Hansel comforted her, as he had done
before, by telling her they need only wait until the moon rose.

"As you know, little sister," he said, "I have thrown bread
crumbs all along the path we traveled, and they will easily
show us the way back home."

But when they went out of the thicket into
the moonlight, they did not find any bread crumbs, for
the many birds that lived in the trees of the forest had
eaten them all up.

Hansel tried to hide his fear, and said to his little sister,
"Cheer up, Gretel. We shall find our way home even without
the bread crumbs. Let's try!" But they could not.

They wandered about the whole night, and the next day
from morning until evening. But they could not find their way
out of the wood. They were so hungry that had it not been for
the few berries they picked, they might have starved.

The children finally grew so tired that their poor little
legs could carry them no farther, so they laid themselves
down under a tree and went to sleep.

When they awoke, it was the third morning since they had left their father's house. They tried again to find their way home, but it was no use. They only walked deeper into the wood. They knew that if no help came, they would soon starve. At midday, they saw a lovely snow-white bird sitting on the branch of a tree. It sang so beautifully that they stood still to listen.

When the bird finished his song, he spread his wings and flew in front of them. The children followed him until at last they saw a small house in the distance. The bird flew up onto the roof.

But how surprised were the boy and girl, when they came near, to find that the house was built of gingerbread, and decorated with sweet cakes and tarts, with windows made of sugar!

"Oh!" exclaimed Hansel. "Let us stop here and have a splendid feast. I will have a piece from the roof first, Gretel, and you can eat some of the sugar window, which will taste so sweet and nice."

Hansel stood on tiptoe and broke off a piece of the gingerbread. He ate with all his might, for he was very hungry. Gretel sat on the doorstep and began munching on a piece of the window. Suddenly, a gentle voice came out of the cottage:

"Nibbling, nibbling like a mouse

Who is eating my little house?"

The children then answered:

"The wind, the wind, only the wind."

And they continued eating as if they never meant to stop. Hansel, who found that the cake on the roof tasted very good, broke off another large piece. Gretel had just taken out a whole pane of sugar from the window and sat down to eat it, when the door opened, and a strange old woman came out.

Hansel and Gretel were so frightened that they dropped the sweets
they held in their hands. But the old woman only shook her head at them and
said, "Ah, you dear children, who has brought you here? Come in and stay
with me for a little while. No harm shall come to you."

Offering them cakes and cookies, she led them into the house. For
supper, the old woman gave them plenty to eat and drink—pancakes and

sugar, milk, apples, and nuts. When evening came, Hansel and Gretel were each given a little bed with white curtains, and when they lay down they felt they were in heaven.

Although the old woman pretended to be friendly and kind, she was really a wicked witch, who had built her house of gingerbread so that she could trap little children. Once they were in her power, she would feed them until they were fat. Then she would cook them for her dinner, which she called her "great feast."

Luckily, the witch had weak eyes, and could not see very well. But she had a very sharp sense of smell, as wild animals have, and could easily tell when human beings were nearby. When Hansel and Gretel walked up to her cottage, she laughed to herself wickedly, and said, with a sneer, "I have them now! They shall not escape from me!"

The witch got up early in the morning, before the children were awake. She stood by their beds and, when she saw how beautiful they looked in their sleep, with their round rosy cheeks, she said to herself, "What dainty morsels they will be!"

Then she grabbed Hansel with her rough hands, dragged him out of bed, led him to a little cage that had bars on the door, and locked him in. He could scream as much as he liked, but she would pay no attention.

Then she went to Gretel's bed and, shaking the girl until she awoke, cried, "Get up, you lazybones, and fetch some water, so I may cook something good for your brother, who is shut up in a cage outside until he gets nice and fat. And then I shall cook him and eat him!"

When Gretel heard this, she began to cry bitterly. But it was no use. She had to do just what the wicked witch told her to do.

The best of everything was cooked for poor Hansel's breakfast. Gretel had nothing to eat but the shell of a crab. Every morning, the old woman would go out to the little cage and say, "Hansel, stick out your finger so I can feel how fat you are." But Hansel, who knew how dim her eyes were, always stuck a bone through the bars of his cage, and the old witch, who could not see, thought it was his finger. Each time she felt how thin it was, she wondered why he did not ever get fat.

As the weeks passed, and Hansel seemed only to grow thinner, the witch became very impatient, until she could not wait any longer.

"Go, Gretel," she cried to the little girl. "Hurry and fetch some water. Hansel may be fat or lean, I don't care. Tomorrow morning, I will cook him and have my feast!"

Oh! How the poor little sister cried as she drew the water from the well. And, as the tears rolled down her cheeks, she said, "It would have been better to be eaten by wild animals, or to have starved to death in the wood. Then, at least, we should have died together!"

"Stop your crying!" said the old witch. "It is not of the least use. No one will come to help you."

Early the next morning, Gretel was forced to fill the great pot with water and hang it over the fire to boil.

When this was done, the old woman said, "We will bake some bread first. I have made the oven hot, and the dough is already kneaded." Then she pulled poor little Gretel close to the oven door, where the flames were burning fiercely. "Creep in there," she said, "and see if it is hot enough to bake the bread."

If Gretel had obeyed her, she would have shut the poor child in and baked her for dinner, instead of boiling Hansel.

But Gretel guessed what the witch wanted to do, and said, "I don't know how to get in through that narrow door."

"Stupid goose," said the witch. "Why, the oven door is quite large enough even for me! Just look, I could get in myself." She stepped forward and pretended to put her head in the oven.

Just then, Gretel gave her a push that sent the old witch right into the oven. Then she shut the iron door and fastened the bolt.

Oh! How the old witch did howl! It was quite horrible to hear her. But Gretel ran away, and left the witch to burn in the oven, just as the witch had left many poor children to burn there before. Gretel ran as fast as she could to Hansel, opened the door of his cage, and cried, "Hansel, Hansel, we are free! The old witch is dead!"

Hansel rushed out, like a bird flying out of its cage when the door is left open. The children were so happy that they ran into each other's arms, kissed each other, and danced about with joy.

And now that there was nothing more to be afraid of, the children went back into the witch's house, and looking around, they saw an old oak chest, which they opened. It was full of pearls and precious stones.

"These are better than pebbles," said Hansel, and he filled his pockets until they could hold no more.

"I will carry some home, too," said Gretel, and she filled her apron, which held quite as much as Hansel's pockets.

"Now we must go," he said, "and get away as soon as we can from this enchanted forest."

They had been walking for nearly two hours when they came to a large body of water.

"What shall we do?" asked Hansel. "We can't get across, and there is no bridge of any sort."

"Oh! Here comes a boat!" cried Gretel, but she was mistaken. It was only a white duck, which came swimming toward the children.

"Perhaps she will help us across if we ask her," said Gretel, who then began to sing out, "Little duck, do help poor Hansel and Gretel. There is not a bridge, nor a boat. Will you let us sail across on your white back?"

The duck came near the bank as Gretel spoke, so close indeed that Hansel could seat himself on its back. He wanted his little sister to sit on his lap, but she said, "No, we will be too heavy for the kind duck. Let her take us across the water one at a time."

The good creature did as the children wished. She carried Hansel over first, and then came back for Gretel. And then how happy the children were to find themselves in a part of the wood that they remembered quite well! As they walked on, the wood grew more and more familiar until at last they caught sight of their father's house. Then they began to run, and, rushing inside, they threw themselves into their father's arms.

Poor man, he had not had a moment's peace since his wife had left his children in the forest. Now he was full of joy at finding them safe and well again. And they had nothing more to fear, for their wicked stepmother had died.

But how surprised the poor woodcutter was when Gretel shook out her little apron and scattered glittering pearls and precious stones about the room, and Hansel pulled handful after handful from his pockets. From this moment, the father's sorrow was at an end, and he lived in happiness with his children for the rest of his long life.

The End

The Frog Prince

In the old days, when it was still of some use to wish for the thing one wanted, there lived a king whose daughters were all beautiful, but the youngest was so beautiful that the sun himself, who had seen so much, lingered each time he shone over her because of her great beauty.

Near the royal castle there was a great dark wood, and in the wood, under an old linden tree, was a well. When the day was hot, the king's daughter would go into the wood and sit by the edge of the cool well, and when she got bored, she would take out a golden ball and throw it up and catch it again, and this was her favorite pastime.

Now, it happened one day that the golden ball, instead of falling back into the maiden's little hand, dropped instead on the edge of the well and rolled in. The king's daughter followed it with her eyes as it sank, but the well was deep, so deep that the bottom could not be seen. Then she began to

weep, and she wept and wept as if she could never be comforted. In the midst of her weeping, she heard a voice say to her, "What is wrong, king's daughter? Your tears would melt a heart of stone."

And when she looked to see where the voice was coming from, she saw nothing but a frog stretching his thick ugly head out of the water.

"Oh, is it you, old waddler?" she said. "I am crying because my golden ball has fallen into the well."

"Never mind, do not weep," answered the frog. "I can help you, but what will you give me if I fetch your ball?"

"Whatever you like, dear frog," she said. "Any of my clothes, my pearls and jewels, or even the golden crown I wear."

"Your clothes, your pearls and jewels, and your golden crown are not for me," answered the frog. "But if you would love me, and have me for your companion and playmate, and let me sit by you at the table, and eat from your plate, and drink from your cup, and sleep in your little bed—if you would promise me all this, then I would gladly dive below the water and return your golden ball to you."

"Oh yes," she answered. "I will promise it all, whatever you want, if you will only get me my ball again." But she thought to herself, "What

nonsense he talks! As if he could do anything but sit in the water and croak with the other frogs, or could possibly be anyone's companion."

But the frog, as soon as he heard her promise, ducked his head under the water and sank down out of sight, and after a while he came to the surface again with the ball in his mouth, and he threw it on the grass beside her. The king's daughter was overjoyed to see her pretty plaything again, and she picked it up and ran off with it.

"Wait, wait!" cried the frog. "Take me with you. I cannot run as fast as you can!"

But it was no use. For "croak, croak" after her as he might, she would not listen to him, but instead hurried home, and very soon forgot all about the poor frog, who had to go back into his well again.

The next day, when the king's daughter was sitting at the table with the king and all the court, and eating from her golden plate, there came something pitter-patter up the marble stairs, and then there came a knocking at the door, and a voice crying, "Yoo-hoo, Princess, let me in!"

She got up and ran to see who it could be, but when she opened the door, there was the frog sitting outside. Then she shut the door hastily and went back to her seat, feeling very uneasy. The king noticed how quickly her heart was beating, and said, "My child, what are you afraid of? Is there a giant standing at the door ready to carry you away?"

"Oh no," she answered, "no giant, but a horrid frog."

"And what does the frog want?" asked the king.

"Oh, dear Father," she answered, "when I was sitting by the well yesterday and playing with my golden ball, it fell into the water, and while I was crying for the loss of it, the frog came and got it again for me on the condition that I would let him be my companion. I never thought that he could leave the water and come after me, but now, there he is outside the door, and he wants to come in to me."

And then they all heard the frog knocking a second time and crying, "Remember me, Princess? I live in the well. Yesterday, your golden ball fell into the well and I offered to help when I heard your crying. So please let me in. Please keep your promise."

"If you have made a promise, my daughter," said the king, "you must keep it. So go now, and let him in."

So the princess went and opened the door, and the frog hopped in, following at her heels, until she reached her chair.

Then he stopped and cried, "Lift me up to sit by you."

But she put off doing it until the king ordered her to. Once the frog was seated on the chair, he wanted to get onto the table, and there he sat and said, "Now push your golden plate a little nearer, so that we may eat together."

And so she did, but everybody could see how unwilling she was, and although the frog feasted heartily, every morsel seemed to stick in her throat.

"I have had enough now," said the frog at last, "and as I am tired, you must carry me to your room, and make ready your silken bed, and we will lie down and go to sleep."

Then the king's daughter began to weep. She was afraid of the cold frog, and knew that nothing would satisfy him but to sleep in her pretty clean bed. The king grew angry with her, saying, "That which you have promised in your time of need, you must now deliver."

So she picked up the frog with her finger and thumb, carried him upstairs, and put him in a corner, and when she had lain down in her bed to sleep, he came creeping up to her, saying, "I am tired and want sleep as much as you. Pick me up, or I will tell your father."

The princess's patience with the frog was nearly at an end. In anger, she picked him up once more and was about to throw him through the doorway. Then, remembering her father's words, she stopped, and dropped him onto the pillow instead.

"Ahh," said the frog, as he snuggled down into the silken sheets. "Don't you love sleepovers?"

The princess, pulling the covers over her head, curled up on the farthest edge of the mattress, with her back to the frog—and went to sleep.

And that is how it went for the next three days and nights. The princess did all the things that a princess usually does, but she was always

accompanied by the little frog. But a strange thing happened during those three days after the princess had made her promise. The princess actually grew fond of the little frog.

On the evening of the third day, the strangest thing of all happened. Before blowing out the candle as they prepared to go to sleep, the princess leaned over and kissed the frog good-night.

In a twinkling, the frog ceased to be a frog at all. He became a handsome young prince with beautiful, kind eyes.

Immediately, the princess and the prince ran downstairs to find the king. The prince told how a wicked witch had imprisoned him in the body of a frog, and that only the love of a princess could release him from the spell.

It was decided on that very day that when the prince and princess came of age, they would marry and join their fortunes and their kingdoms together.

The next day, a grand carriage arrived at the door of the castle. It was drawn by eight white horses with tall white plumes on their heads, and they were wearing harnesses of gold. The carriage was sent by the prince's father, to take the prince and princess back to his kingdom, so they could share the happy news with his family. On the carriage rode Henry, the faithful servant of the young prince.

Henry had been so troubled and saddened when his master was turned into a frog that he found it necessary to wear three iron bands around his heart, to keep it from breaking with grief. Henry was now full of joy to see his master again. After helping the royal pair into the carriage, Henry jumped onto the carriage himself, and they were soon off.

They had not gone very far when the prince heard a cracking sound, as if something were breaking in the back of the carriage. The prince turned and cried, "Henry, the wheel must be breaking!"

"No, my good prince," Henry answered, "it is not the carriage. It is only my heart, which is now so full of happiness at seeing you again, that it breaks the iron bands that have kept it whole for these many years."

Again, and yet once again, the same cracking sound was heard as the remaining bands broke away from faithful Henry's joyful heart.

The End

Rumplestiltskin

here was once a miller who was very poor, but he had a very beautiful daughter. Now, it happened one day that he had occasion to speak with the king, and in order to give himself an air of importance, the miller said, "I have a daughter who can spin gold out of straw."

So the king said to the miller, "That is an art in which I am much interested. If your daughter is as skillful as you say she is, bring her to my castle tomorrow, and I will put her to the test."

The next day, when the girl was brought to the castle, the king took her to a chamber that was quite full of straw and gave her a spinning wheel.

"Now set to work," he said, "and if between tonight and tomorrow at dawn you have not spun this straw into gold, you must die."

Then the king carefully locked the door of the chamber, and she remained alone.

There sat the unfortunate miller's daughter, and for the life of her she did not know what to do. She had not the least idea how to spin straw into gold, and she became more and more distressed, until at last she began to cry.

All at once, the door sprang open, and in stepped a little man, who said, "Good evening, Mistress Miller. What are you weeping so for?"

"Alas!" answered the maiden. "I've got to spin gold out of straw, and I don't know how to do it."

Then the little man said, "What will you give me if I spin it for you?"

"My necklace," said the maiden.

The little man agreed. He sat down at the spinning wheel, and *whir-whir-whir*, in an instant, the reel was full. Then he put on another reel, and *whir-whir-whir*, three times around, and that, too, was full. And so it went on until morning, when all the straw was spun, and all the reels full of gold. With that, the little man took the necklace and disappeared.

Immediately at sunrise, the king came into the chamber, and when he saw the piles of glittering gold, he was surprised and much pleased. But the sight made him even more greedy. So he had his guards take the miller's daughter to another chamber, much larger than the first one, and also full of straw, and he again ordered her to spin all the straw into gold in one night, if she valued her life.

The maiden was at her wit's end and she began to weep. Once again, the door sprang open, and the little man appeared.

"What will you give me if I spin the straw into gold for you?" he asked.

"The ring off my finger," answered the maiden.

The little man took the ring, began to whir again at the wheel, and had, by morning, spun all the straw into gold.

The king was delighted at the sight of the piles of gold, but was still not satisfied. He had the miller's daughter taken to an even larger chamber, full of straw, and said, "Tonight you must spin all this into gold, and if you succeed, you shall become my queen."

"Even if she is only a miller's daughter," he thought, "I won't find a richer woman in the whole world."

When the young girl was alone, the little man
came to her again and said for the third time, "What will
you give me if I spin the straw for you this time?"
"I have nothing more that I can give," answered the maiden.
"Well, promise me your first child if you become queen."
"Who knows what may happen?" thought the miller's
daughter. She didn't know what else to do, so she promised the little
man what he asked, and again he spun the straw into gold.

When the king arrived in the morning, and found everything done as he had wished, he soon kept his promise and married the miller's daughter, and she became queen.

When one year had passed, a beautiful child was born to the queen, but by that time she had forgotten all about the little man. One day, however, he suddenly entered the queen's chamber, and said, "Now you must give me what you have promised."

The queen was terrified, and she offered the little man all the wealth of the kingdom if he would let her keep the child.

"No," he said. "I would rather have some living thing than all the treasures in the world."

Then the queen began to moan and weep so much that the little man's heart softened and he felt sorry for her.

"I will give you three days," he said, "and if, within that time, you discover my name, you may keep the child."

During the night, the queen tried to remember all the names that she had ever heard, and she sent a messenger all over the country to ask far and wide what other names there were.

When the little man came the next day, she began with Caspar, Melchior, Balthasar, and mentioned all the names she knew, one after the other. But at every one the little man said, "No, that's not my name."

On the second day, she asked all around the neighborhood for the names of people living there, and then suggested to the little man all the most unusual and strange names.

"Perhaps your name is Cowribs, Spindleshanks, or Lacelegs?"

But he answered every time, "No, that's not my name."

On the third day, the queen's messenger returned to the castle. "I haven't been able to find any new names," he said, "but as I came around the corner of a wood on a lofty mountain, where the fox says 'good night' to the hare, I saw a little house, and in front of the house a fire was burning, and around the fire, an indescribably ridiculous little man was leaping, and hopping on one leg, and singing:

"Today I bake. Tomorrow I brew my beer.

The next day I will bring the queen's child here.

Ah! Lucky it is that not a soul does know

That Rumplestiltskin is my name! Ho! Ho!"

Now, you can imagine how delighted the queen was when she heard the name, and when, soon afterward, the little man came in and asked, "Now, Your Majesty, what is my name?"

At first she asked, "Is your name Kunz?"

"No."

"Is it Heinz?"

"No."

"Is it, by chance, Rumplestiltskin?"

"The devil told you that! The devil told you that!" shrieked the little man in a rage. He stamped his right foot into the ground so deep that he sank up to his waist. Then he jumped up and flew out of the window, riding on a cooking spoon.

The End

Cinderella

Once upon a time, there was an honest man who took for his second wife the proudest and most unpleasant woman that had ever been seen. She had two daughters, who had their mother's temper and resembled her in every other way. Her husband, on the other hand, had a young daughter who had a very sweet and gentle nature. She resembled her own dead mother, who had been the nicest person in the world.

The wedding was no sooner over than the stepmother began to show the signs of her bad temper. She was jealous of the good qualities of her young stepdaughter, for they made her own daughters seem more hateful than ever. She gave the young girl all the most difficult tasks about the house.

She had to wash the floors and staircases, clean the plates, and sweep out the rooms of the mistress of the house and her daughters. She slept on an old straw mattress in the attic at the top of the house, while the sisters had rooms with carpets and beds of the most fashionable style, and ornate mirrors in which they regularly admired themselves.

The poor girl suffered all in silence, not daring to complain to her father.
He would surely have scolded her, because he was ruled by his new wife.

When the girl had finished her daily work, she would sit among the
cinders in the corner of the fireplace. Because of this, she often looked dirty,
and the younger of the two stepsisters, who was not quite as cruel as the
other, called the girl Cinderella. But her shabby clothes did not prevent
Cinderella from being a hundred times more beautiful than her stepsisters,
for all their fine clothing.

It happened that the king's son was giving a great ball, and he invited all the young ladies in the kingdom to attend, so that he might choose one as his future bride. But he did not invite Cinderella, because he had never seen or heard of her.

When the two stepsisters received their invitations to the prince's ball, they were very proud and happy, and spent all of their time deciding what clothes would be most flattering to them, and how they should style their hair. And all this activity meant more trouble for Cinderella, for she had to iron their fine linens and press their ruffles and laces. The stepsisters could talk of nothing else but the ball.

"For my part," said the elder stepsister, "I shall wear my dress of red velvet, with the fine English lace."

"I have only my everyday silk petticoat," said the younger, "but, to make up for it, I shall wear my cloak with the golden flowers and my necklace of diamonds, which is quite fine."

They called for Cinderella and asked her advice, too, for she had very good taste. Cinderella gave them the best possible suggestions and even offered to fix their hair, to which they gladly agreed. While she was combing their hair, they said:

"Cinderella, don't you wish that you were going to the ball?"

"Ah, but you fine young ladies are laughing at me. That would surely be no place for a plain girl like me."

"That is very true," the sisters said. "People would laugh to see a dirty cindermaiden in the ballroom!"

Anyone else but Cinderella would have messed their hair, but she was good-natured, and she fixed it even and smooth, and made it as pretty as she could.

The stepsisters were so excited that they broke more than a dozen laces by drawing them too tight, to make their waists appear more slender, and they constantly stood looking at themselves in front of the mirror.

At last, the happy day arrived. Away the stepsisters went, and Cinderella watched them for as long as she could keep them in sight. When she could no longer see their coach, she began to cry.

Immediately, her godmother, who was a fairy, appeared beside her. She saw her tears and asked, "Why are you crying, my dear girl?"

"Oh, I should like, I should like . . ." She was crying so bitterly that she could not finish the sentence.

"You would like to go the ball, wouldn't you?" asked her fairy godmother.

"Ah, yes," said Cinderella, sighing.

"Well, well," said her godmother. "Promise to be a good girl and I will arrange for you to go."

Then she led Cinderella outside and said, "Go into the garden and bring me the largest pumpkin you can find."

Cinderella went at once and picked the largest pumpkin that she could find, wondering how a pumpkin could ever get her to the ball. Her godmother scooped it out, and when only the rind was left, she struck it with her wand. Instantly, the pumpkin changed into a beautiful coach, lined with rose-colored satin.

Then she asked Cinderella to fetch the mousetrap from the pantry. Inside, there were six mice, all still alive.

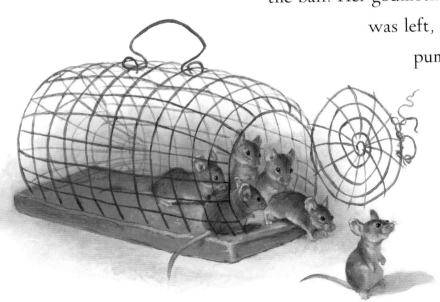

The fairy godmother opened the
wire door, and as each mouse came out,
she gave it a tap with her wand and
changed it into a fine horse, so that there
was a team of six dappled mouse-gray horses.

"But what shall I do for your coachman,
Cinderella?" she asked.

"I will go and see if there is a rat in the rattrap," said Cinderella.
"We could make a coachman of him."

"Quite right," said her godmother. "Go and see."

Cinderella brought in the rattrap, which contained three large rats.
The fairy godmother chose one with elegant whiskers.

As soon as she touched him, he turned
into a fat coachman with the finest
mustache that ever was seen.

"Now go into the garden, Cinderella, and bring
me the two lizards that you will find behind the
well." No sooner had she brought them than the fairy godmother turned them into
footmen, who at once climbed up behind the coach in their braided uniforms and
hung on there as if they had never done anything else all their lives.

"Well, Cinderella, now you are ready to go to the ball!"

"Oh," she replied, "but am I to go in these ragged clothes?"

The fairy godmother lightly touched Cinderella with her wand and, in
an instant, her ragged clothes were changed into garments of gold and silver
cloth, sparkling with jewels. Then her godmother gave her a pair of glass
slippers, the prettiest in all the world.

Cinderella entered the splendid coach.
Her godmother said, "Now, Cinderella, be on
your way. But remember, if you stay one minute
past midnight, your coach will again become a
pumpkin, your horses mice, and your footmen
lizards. And you will look like a cindermaiden
again in your old, ragged clothes."

Cinderella promised that she would not
fail to leave the ball before midnight, and away
she went, her heart filled with delight.

As Cinderella's coach arrived at the palace,
a buzz of excitement filled the air. Gracefully
stepping from the carriage, she glided through
the entryway and into the great hall.

At once, there fell a great silence. The
dancers stopped, the violins played no more,
so fixed was everyone's attention on the great
beauty of the unknown guest. Everywhere
could be heard, in confused whispers, "Oh,
how beautiful she is!"

The king, old man though he
was, could not take his eyes off her and
whispered to the queen that it was

many a long day since he had seen anyone so beautiful and charming.

All the ladies were eager to study her clothes and her hair, determined to copy the style the very next day, if they could find fabrics as fine and tailors as clever.

The young prince placed Cinderella in the seat of honor and then led her by the hand to dance with him. Such was the grace with which she danced, that the admiration of all the guests grew even greater.

A magnificent supper was served, but the young prince ate nothing, as he was so busy watching Cinderella. She went to sit beside her stepsisters and asked them to share with her the oranges and lemons that the king had given her, which greatly surprised and delighted them, for they did not recognize her at all.

While they were talking, Cinderella heard the clock strike a quarter to twelve. She at once made a deep curtsy and said farewell and departed as quickly as she could.

When Cinderella arrived home, she found her fairy godmother waiting for her. Cinderella thanked her for all she had done, and asked if she could attend the ball again the next day, as the king's son had invited her.

While she was busy telling her godmother all that had happened, her two stepsisters knocked at her door. The fairy godmother vanished, and Cinderella let them in.

"What a long time you have been away this evening!" Cinderella said, rubbing her eyes and stretching, as if she had only just awakened.

"If you had been at the ball," said one of the sisters, "you would not be feeling weary at all. There arrived a most beautiful princess, the most beautiful that anyone has ever seen, and she was very polite to us both and let us share her oranges and lemons."

Cinderella was overjoyed. She asked them the name of the princess, but they replied that no one knew it and that the king's son was so in love that he would give anything in the world to know who she was. Cinderella smiled and said she must have been beautiful indeed.

"Oh, how lucky you are!" she said. "Couldn't I see her, too? Oh, please, Javotte, lend me the yellow dress that you wear every day so that I may go to the ball!"

"Indeed!" said the elder stepsister, Javotte. "This is a fine idea. Lend my dress to a dirty cindermaiden like you. You must think I am crazy!"

Cinderella had expected her stepsister to say this. She was not at all upset, for she was asking to wear the dress in jest and did not really want to wear it at all.

The next night, the two stepsisters again went to the ball, and Cinderella, even more splendidly dressed than she was the first time, followed them a short time after.

All night long, the king's
son stayed close by her and paid her endless
compliments. The young girl was enjoying herself so much
that she completely forgot her fairy godmother's warning, and when
the first stroke of midnight fell upon her ears, she thought it was not more
than eleven o'clock.

She rose and fled as nimbly as a fawn. The prince followed her, but
could not catch her. As she ran, she lost one of her glass slippers, and the
prince picked it up with tender care.

When Cinderella arrived home, she was out of breath, without coach or
footmen, and in her old, shabby dress. Nothing remained of her splendid clothes
except one of the little glass slippers, the mate to the one that she had lost.

The prince asked the guards at the palace gate if they had seen a
princess go out, but they said they had seen no one leave except a young girl
in ragged clothes, who looked more like a peasant than a young lady.

When her two stepsisters returned from the ball, Cinderella asked them
if they had enjoyed themselves and if the beautiful lady had again been there.

They told her that she had, but fled away at midnight and in such haste
that she lost one of her little glass slippers.

They told her that the king's son picked it up, and did nothing but
gaze at it for the rest of the ball, and that most certainly he was deeply
in love with its beautiful owner.

What the stepsisters said was true. A few days later, the prince announced, with the sound of trumpets, that he would take for his wife the maiden whose foot would fit the glass slipper. All the princesses, then all the duchesses, and then the whole of the court tried on the slipper, but it fit no one.

Finally, the king's men brought the glass slipper to the home of the two stepsisters, who each did all that she could to squeeze her foot into the tiny slipper. But they could not.

Cinderella was looking on and saw right away that this was her slipper. "May I please see if it will fit me?" she asked.

Her sisters burst out laughing and began to make fun of her, but the king's servant looked closely at Cinderella. Seeing that she was very beautiful, he said that she should indeed try the glass slipper, as the prince had commanded that every maiden in the city try it on.

The servant asked Cinderella to sit down, and as soon as he put the slipper on her little foot, he saw that it slid on without trouble and was molded to her exact shape like wax.

The two stepsisters were greatly surprised at this, and they were even more surprised when Cinderella drew from her pocket the matching glass slipper, which she also put on. At that very moment, her fairy godmother appeared. She gave a tap with her wand to Cinderella's clothes and changed them into a dress even more splendid than any of the others.

The two stepsisters now recognized her as the beautiful person they had seen at the ball and they threw themselves at her feet, begging her forgiveness for all their cruelty toward her. Cinderella raised them up, and embraced them, saying that she forgave them with all her heart, and asking that they love her well from that day forward.

Cinderella was taken to the palace of the young prince, dressed as she was in her fine new clothes. He found her more beautiful than ever, and a few days later, they were married.

Cinderella, who was as good as she was beautiful, invited her step-sisters to live in the palace with her, and married them the very same day to two noble gentlemen of the court.

The End

Three Little Pigs

Once upon a time, when pigs spoke in rhyme, and monkeys chewed tobacco, and hens took snuff to make them tough, and ducks went "quack, quack, quack, oh!" there was an old sow who had three little pigs. Now, this wise mother pig knew that the time had come for her children to be out on their own. And even though it saddened her greatly to do so, she packed each one a lunch and sent the three little pigs off to seek their fortunes.

Tiny eyes wept salty tears as the little pigs left the homey comforts of trough and sty. With a final oink and sob, each walked through the gate and out into the wide world.

The first little pig to leave home soon met a man on the road who was carrying a load of straw. "Please, Mr. Man, will you give me that straw, so that I can build myself a house?" asked the pig.

The man did so, and the pig set to work, building himself a house of straw. When he had finished, he was quite pleased with himself and sat in the shade of a tree to enjoy his lunch. Suddenly, a wolf came down the road and, in an instant, the little pig was inside his house. As the door bolt snapped shut, the pig breathed a sigh of relief.

But then there was a loud knock on the door, and he heard the wolf say, "Little pig, little pig, let me come in!"

To which the pig answered, "Not by the hair of my chinny-chin-chin!"

"Well!" said the wolf, showing his teeth. "Then I'll huff, and I'll puff, and I'll blow your house in!"

Then the wolf huffed and he puffed, and he blew the house in. Luckily, the little pig safely scrambled through the swirling straw and quickly ran off across the countryside.

Meanwhile, the second little pig had met a man on the road who was carrying a bundle of sticks.

"Please, Mr. Man," the little pig said, "will you give me that bundle of sticks, so that I can build myself a house?"

The man did so, and the pig set to work at once, building himself a house of sticks. When he had finished, he made himself a hammock and lay in the shade to enjoy his lunch.

Suddenly, his brother appeared, running up the hill, waving his arms and crying that the wolf was close behind him.

No sooner had the two little pigs scrambled into the house of sticks than, indeed, the wolf appeared.

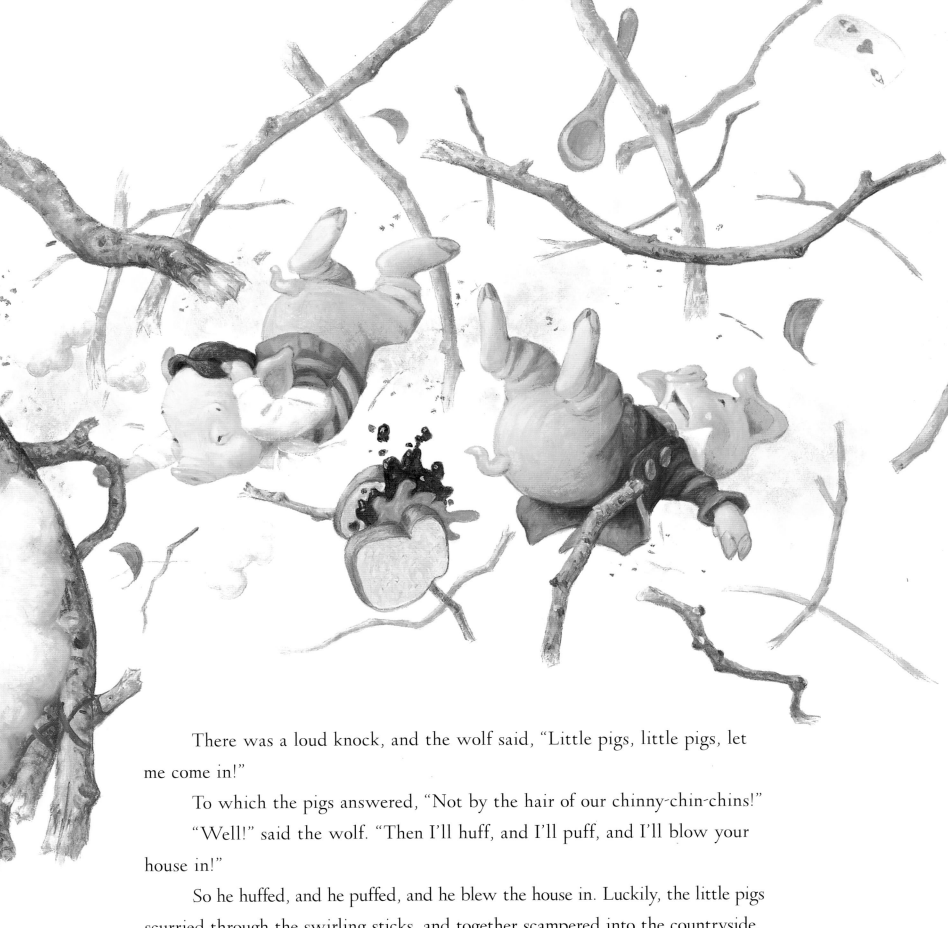

There was a loud knock, and the wolf said, "Little pigs, little pigs, let me come in!"

To which the pigs answered, "Not by the hair of our chinny-chin-chins!"

"Well!" said the wolf. "Then I'll huff, and I'll puff, and I'll blow your house in!"

So he huffed, and he puffed, and he blew the house in. Luckily, the little pigs scurried through the swirling sticks, and together scampered into the countryside.

Meanwhile, the third little pig had met a man on the road who was carrying a load of bricks.

"Please, Mr. Man," the little pig said, "will you give me those bricks, so that I can build myself a house?"

The man did so, and the little pig immediately set to work, building himself a house of bricks. When he had finished, he was quite happy with himself and sat down to enjoy his lunch before beginning to dig his garden.

Suddenly, his little brothers could be seen running down the road, waving their arms and calling him.

"Drop the hoe! Do not stay! The wolf will blow your house away!"

But the third little pig said, "Come inside, double-quick! My little house is made of brick!" In a moment, all three little pigs stood behind the locked door of the brick house.

And indeed, after a very short time, the wolf appeared. There was a loud knock at the door, and he said, "Little pigs, little pigs, let me come in."

To which the pigs replied, "Not by the hair of our chinny-chin-chins!"

"Well," said the wolf. "Then I'll huff, and I'll puff, and I'll blow your house in!"

So he huffed, and he puffed, and he puffed, and he huffed, but he soon learned that with all of his huffing and puffing, he could not so much as even loosen a shingle off the little pig's brick house.

"Little pigs," said the wolf, catching his breath, "I know where there is a wonderful field of turnips."

"Really," said the third pig, "is that so? Please tell us where so we can go!"

"Oh," said the wolf, smiling to himself, "in Mr. Smith's field. If you would like, I will come by tomorrow morning, and we can walk over there together."

With a wink and a smile to his brothers, the pig replied, "I was wrong. You're a nice guy. Just let me know what time you'll drop by."

"Let's make it six o'clock," said the wolf, and he slinked off down the road.

Well, the little pigs got up at five, went out, picked the turnips, and returned home just before the wolf arrived.

"Ready to go?" the wolf asked sweetly through the closed door.

"Ready? Heck, we're all done! We got up before the sun," laughed the little pigs.

The wolf's eyes widened, and he gritted his teeth in anger, but being a sly fellow, he held his breath and waited a moment. Then, as sweetly as before, he said, "Well, little pigs, let's not dwell on the past. I know of a wonderful apple tree nearby. Why don't we all go over there and pick apples together?"

"Delightful, yes! Let's go! Tell us where, so we will know!" said the third little pig.

"At Merry Garden," said the wolf. "So no tricks now, and I'll see you at five."

Well, once again, the third little pig got his brothers out of bed an hour earlier, and they headed off to pick apples, hoping to get back before the wolf arrived at their door.

But the wolf was not so easily fooled this time, and the pigs saw him coming while they were still high in the tree.

"Little pigs, what a surprise to find you here so early," said the wolf, smiling. "Tell me, are the apples good?"

"Good? They're great!" called the third little pig. "I'll toss one down, if you'll just wait!"

And so he did, but the apple went over the wolf's head and rolled into the bushes, and the wolf ran off to find it.

In a twinkling, the pigs climbed down from the tree, and they were halfway home before the wolf realized that he had been tricked again.

Later, back at the pig's front door, the wolf had another outing in mind.

"Little pigs, what a shame we keep missing each other," said the wolf. "There is a fair in Shinklin this afternoon. What do you say we walk over together and spend the day?"

They agreed to meet at one o'clock.

So once again, the pigs set out much earlier than arranged. They went to the fair and bought a butter churn. On the way home, the pigs had just carried it to the top of a hill when they saw the wolf coming.

Not knowing what else to do, they climbed inside of the churn and rolled down the hill.

The sight and sound of the wooden churn rolling toward him so frightened the wolf that he ran home without ever going to the fair.

Later, at the pig's house, the wolf told the three little pigs how he had been frightened on the road by a rolling butter churn.

"Ha-ha, old wolf, for a fool you've been taken. That butter churn was full of bacon!"

The wolf could hear the little pigs rolling on the floor in laughter. His patience was at an end. Leaping onto the roof, he shouted, "Enough is enough, little pigs! Tonight you shall be my supper!"

Immediately, the third little pig realized that the wolf was planning to come down the chimney. Placing a pot of boiling water over the fire, he stood back to wait. As the first bits of chimney soot fell onto the pot, the little pig removed the cover.

Suddenly, the wolf came down the chimney and landed in the bubbling water with a splash. In an instant, the little pig replaced the cover and boiled the wolf up.

That evening, the three little pigs danced and sang, and dined on wolf stew, which was the custom in those days. They lived very happily in that little brick house, and perhaps they are living there still.

The End

A Note from the Illustrator

This book represents for me the longest ongoing project that I have ever undertaken. The initial ten paintings were commissioned for a series of collector's plates and limited-edition prints, and I intended to use those pieces as the foundation for an illustrated fairy tales book. Little did I realize that twelve years would elapse, with many other projects and pictures, before the additional sixty-five fairy tales paintings would be completed and this book would finally become a reality.

All of these pictures began life as sketches. Sometimes it took as many as six to eight quick sketches before I discovered the best composition. The sketch was then used as a basis for gathering reference material such as books on costumes, furniture, architecture, and other artists' works from appropriate periods—as well as a guide for posing models. The models were usually photographed in costume and acting out a scene in the story.

Next, I made a pencil drawing using these photographs, along with the original quick sketch and information from the reference materials. Once the drawing was complete, it was transferred onto a gessoed Masonite panel, where I used it as a guide, painting over it to create the finished work. Some of the largest and most complex paintings took up to three months to complete, whereas simpler pieces may have taken as few as three days.

The creation of these pictures constituted some of my most enjoyable hours in front of an easel, so it seems very appropriate to thank some of the people who helped make these pictures possible. My models are relatives, friends, and neighbors—all of whom I am indebted to for their patience and good humor. They are, in alphabetical order: Kiera Behlow; Chrissie Calkins; Frank Cavello; Michael Dobbs; Kori Edens; Gary Gianni; Tom and Karen Gianni; Karl and Patty Gustafson; Maynard and Wayne Gustafson; Annie, Charlie, and Jack Hoeg; Joan Jones; Shelton Key; Stacy Laya; Hugh Martin; Allan Monroe; Jane Olson; Brittany Owen; Elliot Purse; Carol and Phill Renaud; Eleanor Sandford; Rena Schergen; Cindy Tegtmeyer; Elizabeth and Jerry Tiritilli; Charlotte and Paul Tyler; Blaine Vedros; Dawn Westergard; Jennifer Willison; and John Zielinski.

Beyond the physical presence and goodwill that the models contributed to these pictures, there were others, working behind the scenes, who played a part in various stages of this project. Those at the Bradford Exchange were John McKinven, Cathy Bogaert, and Lauren Guttenberg. David Usher and Jennifer Oakes at the Greenwich Workshop provided early encouragement and support, and a very special thanks to their colleagues Wendy Wentworth and Scott Usher, whose belief in the project helped to turn a dream into a reality.

And last but not least, my heartfelt thanks and appreciation to my wife, Patty, and son, Karl, for their love, support, and help from "Once upon a time . . ." to ". . . happily ever after."